# FIVE Little MONKEYS
## go shopping

*For Linda Cassidy
and her first-grade monkeys*

ISBN-13: 978-0-545-11601-5
ISBN-10: 0-545-11601-5

Copyright © 2007 by Eileen Christelow.
All rights reserved. Published by Scholastic Inc., 557 Broadway, New York, NY 10012, by arrangement with Houghton Mifflin Harcourt Publishing Company. SCHOLASTIC and associated logos are trademarks and/or registered trademarks of Scholastic Inc.

12 11 10 9 8 7 6 5 4 3 2          8 9 10 11 12 13/0

Printed in the U.S.A.          40

First Scholastic printing, September 2008

The illustrations were executed in digital pen and ink and acrylic gouache.
The text was set in 18-point Cantoria.

# FIVE Little MONKEYS
## go shopping

EILEEN CHRISTELOW

SCHOLASTIC INC.
New York Toronto London Auckland Sydney
Mexico City New Delhi Hong Kong Buenos Aires

The day before school starts, Mama takes her five little monkeys shopping for clothes. "Stick with me," she says, "and don't go wandering off!"

"We need dresses, pants, shirts, hats, and backpacks for my five little monkeys," says Mama.

4

"But I see only four little monkeys," says the saleslady.

"1 2 3 4."

"You four little monkeys try on these clothes while I go find her. But stay right here, and DON'T GO WANDERING OFF!"

So one little monkey tries on pants.
Two little monkeys try on shirts.
One little monkey tries on a dress.

Then two of those monkeys are so thirsty! They want to find a water fountain.

Off they go . . . just as Mama comes back with the one missing monkey.

"Now I have my five little monkeys!" Mama says.
"But I see only three little monkeys," says the saleslady.

"1 2 3."

"Only three little monkeys?" gasps Mama.
"Am I missing more monkeys?
How can that be?"

"I need to find those two little monkeys!" says Mama. "You three little monkeys can try on more clothes, but STAY RIGHT HERE, AND DON'T GO WANDERING OFF!"

So those three little monkeys are looking for more clothes when they see three monkey friends.

Then one of the little
monkeys needs to find
a bathroom.

Off he goes . . . just as Mama hurries back with her two missing monkeys. "Now I have my five little monkeys," she says.

"But I see seven little monkeys," says the saleslady.

"1 2 3 4 5 6 7."

"Seven little monkeys?" gasps Mama. "How can that be?"

"We found three friends!" two of her little monkeys explain. "Their papa has gone to look for their two little sisters!"

"Oh, no!" says Mama.
"I'm so confused! Am I STILL
missing a monkey?"

7 little monkeys
- 3 friends
———————
= 4 of MY little
monkeys

"I need to find my one little monkey," says Mama. "You seven little monkeys try on more clothes. STAY RIGHT HERE, AND DON'T GO WANDERING OFF!"

But the four little monkeys and their three monkey friends get tired of trying on clothes. "Let's go help Mama!" they say.

Off they go . . . just as Mama hurries
back with her one missing monkey,
the monkey friends' papa, and
their two little sister monkeys.

"Now we have ten little monkeys," says Mama.
"But I see only three little monkeys," says the saleslady.

"1 2 3."

23

"Oh, no!" wails Mama. "Am I still missing some monkeys? How can that be?"

"STAY RIGHT HERE!" says the saleslady. "AND DON'T GO WANDERING OFF!"

Then the saleslady makes an announcement. "Will all the little monkeys who are missing their mamas, papas, little sisters or brothers please come to the children's clothing department RIGHT NOW!"

Lots of little monkeys
hurry to the children's
clothing department.

"Now I have my five little monkeys," says Mama.
"And I have my five little monkeys," says the monkey friends' papa. "So we have ten little monkeys!"

"No," says the saleslady.

"You have fourteen little monkeys.

1 2 3 4 5 6 7 8 9 10 11 12 13 14.

You have four extra little monkeys."

"Those four belong to me!"
cries a grandma monkey.

29

"Now that everyone has found everybody, would anyone like to buy anything?" asks the saleslady.

The five little monkeys and Mama buy dresses, pants, hats, shorts, backpacks, and sunglasses, and then they head for the car.

"At last, we've finished our shopping," says Mama.
"And at last, I have all of my five little monkeys!"

"No, you have six," says one little monkey.

"1 2 3 4 5 6."

How can THAT be?

SCREECH!